Blitz Boys

For Adèle Geras – of course

Blitz Boys

Linda Newbery

A & C Black • London

WORLD WAR II FLASHBACKS

Blood and Ice • Neil Tonge
Final Victory • Herbie Brennan
Blitz Boys • Linda Newbery
The Right Moment • David Belbin

Published 2000 by A & C Black (Publishers) Ltd
35 Bedford Row, London WC1R 4JH

Text copyright © 2000 Linda Newbery

ISBN 0-7136-5421-X

A CIP catalogue record for this book is available
from the British Library.

Printed and bound in Great Britain by
Creative Print & Design (Wales), Ebbw Vale.

Contents

Contents

1 ✣ Trespassing

Ronnie shouldn't be here. He knew that. But then, the other boy shouldn't be here either.

They stared at each other warily, across a pile of rubble. Neither spoke. Then the other boy held out something in his hand. "I found this."

Ronnie looked. It was a child's toy – a wooden horse, painted a glossy dark brown, like a conker. Part of the wooden tail was chipped off, and both ears; eyes stared glassily from its scratched face.

"You can have it, if you want," the boy said. His eyes held Ronnie's, pleading.

"No, thanks. It's just a kid's toy." Ronnie turned away, craning his neck at the upper floor, where a bath stuck out crazily into empty space.

The other boy looked too, and laughed. "Imagine having a bath in that! You'd have to be a bit careful, getting out – "

Ronnie's house didn't have a bath. He shifted his feet on brick fragments and slates. Standing here was both indoors and not-indoors. Beyond the cracked-open bathroom he could see the sky – late-summer blue, with big heaped clouds. But he was inside someone's house, what was left of it. Bomb-ruins were fascinating, as long as it wasn't your house that had been bombed.

There was flowered wallpaper, two different designs, and a tattered curtain had snagged on a protruding pipe. Bits of smashed furniture were scattered around the ground floor, and chunks of bricks and cement and plaster, all covered with a fine powdery dust. He could smell it, taste it in his mouth. The dust got everywhere.

He glanced back at the other boy, who stood with one grey sock sagging around his ankles. He was still holding the horse. When he saw Ronnie watching him, he compressed his lips and chucked it into the rubble. His eyes followed it where it fell, by a fireplace.

Ronnie began picking his way carefully towards the back door. It tilted at an angle, the frame sagging, but there was enough space to get through into the tiny square of garden. The other boy followed.

"I wonder if there are – you know – bodies?"

"No," Ronnie said matter-of-factly. "If there were, they'd have been dug out by now. Unless they're really deep. But look." Ducking through the back door, he pointed towards the humped earth in the back garden, to the corrugated steel structure beneath and the improvised steps that led down to the entrance. "Their Anderson's still here. If they were in there, they'd have been all right. They're supposed to take anything except a direct hit, aren't they?"

The boy made a sound that could have been relief or disappointment. Ronnie looked at him properly for the first time. He looked about twelve, Ronnie's age, but was taller and skinnier. He wore grey shorts and a grey knitted pullover and a dirty white shirt. His hair was fair and untidy, and he had a thin face with anxious blue eyes.

"D'you live round here, then?" Ronnie asked.

"Over there." The boy waved an arm vaguely.

"Where? You're not at my school, are you? Victoria Road?"

Daft question, really, because Victoria Road School was no longer in Victoria Road, but had moved out to safety in Devon, with all its teachers. Ronnie had spent two weeks there – like a holiday, it seemed now – till Mum had brought him back home. The family must stick together, she said, through whatever Hitler threw at them.

The boy shook his head and swallowed. "No. I'm staying with someone. Look, you haven't seen me here, right?"

Ronnie shrugged. "Fine with me. 'S long as you haven't seen me either."

He went back into the house to see if there was anything worth taking. Bits of shrapnel were no longer a novelty – a nose cone from a bomb would be worth having, though who could he show it to, with Chalky and his other friends all hundreds of miles away in Devon?

Still, maybe he might find a clock, a photograph in a frame, silver candlesticks, something he could sell to one of the market stallholders – you never knew. Mum would have given him an ear-bashing if she knew he took stuff – looting, she called it. But Ronnie's reasoning was that the occupiers – if they'd survived – had already had time to come back and take away what they wanted in a wheelbarrow. It was a common enough sight, in the streets – someone trundling along with a barrow heaped high with whatever they could salvage of their possessions.

"There was a UXB here till the day before yesterday," Ronnie said; then, when there was no answer, "You know, an unexploded bomb.

We couldn't have come in here then. They got it out last night."

His voice echoed emptily from the standing walls. He moved back towards the kitchen, then out into the garden. The boy had gone.

* * * * *

To Patsy, Ronnie's little sister, it must seem that there had always been a war – if she could make any sense at all of the disturbed nights, the sirens, the sudden dashes to the Anderson shelter in the garden. Ronnie was still getting used to the strange freedom of not being at school. Officially, he was supposed to have lessons every afternoon in a small room off the church hall, but often the class didn't take place because the tutor couldn't get there or the room was being used for something else – everywhere you went, these days, there were mobile canteens or first-aid centres and people queuing for attention. Ronnie wasn't too particular about turning up. The class was an odd assortment of children of various ages who hadn't been evacuated, and he guessed that the lessons were more to keep them out of trouble than for any other reason. He showed his face often enough to be able to answer with some sort of truthfulness when his mum or dad asked about his school-work. Mostly, they were too busy with their own work – Dad as a post-office sorter by day, air-raid warden by night, and Mum cooking meals at the rest centre.

It was lonely, that was the worst thing. All his friends were in Devon – Chalky, and Jonno, and Ken. There wasn't much for Ronnie to do apart from roam around. Nobody took much notice of him – at twelve he was young enough not to have responsibilities, old enough to be able to take care of himself. If there was a daylight raid, he went to the nearest shelter, or down into the Underground. He liked the Underground – the other world of tunnels under the city, like mole-runs. Now that the bombers were coming nearly every night, some people seemed to stay down there permanently. There was a white line painted all the way along the platform and they had to keep themselves and their blankets and baggage on the wall side of it, so that they didn't get in the way of passengers getting on and off the trains. They were like campers, sitting it out. Mum refused to let the family go there, even though it was probably the safest place to be. "It's unhygienic, all those people crammed together! And what if you needed the toilet? D'you know what they have to use? Buckets! No, you're not getting me down there, not in a month of Sundays." But Ronnie was fascinated by the Underground-dwellers, living like moles in their underworld, rarely coming up for air or daylight. Sometimes he rode on the trains from station to station just to see them.

Roaming around was far more fun if you went where you weren't supposed to go. Ronnie's dad, responsible for Air-Raid Precautions in his patch of the East End, had hauled Ronnie out by the shirt–tails the first time he'd gone into a bombed-out ruin. Then, in the street for everyone to hear, he yelled: "Get indoors, bonehead! Don't you realise all this lot could come crashing round your ears? D'you think the rescue services need more work, digging you out when that happens? Haven't they got enough to do?"

"Sorry, Dad," Ronnie mumbled.

Dad cuffed his arm exasperatedly, and he knew he was forgiven. "Get along home, son. Your nan'd be glad of the company."

Ronnie didn't mean to be a nuisance; he really didn't. What he wanted was to find an unexploded bomb, all by himself. He wanted to be a hero.

2 ✤ In the Anderson

The raid that night was a bad one. Dad, when he came home at tea-time, had said that they must sleep out in the Anderson every night, not wait for the siren, which only gave you a couple of minutes' warning. No one liked it; the shelter was small and dark and smelled of mustiness and feet and wet sandbags, and since it had rained there were two inches of water in the bottom. Mum and Nan sat perched on wooden seats; Ronnie and Patsy had benches made by Dad from planks, the idea being that they might carry on sleeping – as if anyone could! The Anderson might give protection from anything except a direct hit, but it couldn't keep out the noise.

The whole shelter shook to a thunderous explosion to the south. Ronnie clutched at the side of his bench. The hurricane lantern swooped dramatically from its hook, making Nan's shadow loom huge against the wall like something you might see from a ghost train at the fair.

"The docks," Nan said knowledgeably. She hadn't even stopped knitting. "That's what they're going for tonight."

It was no reason to feel complacent. Coronation Road was close enough to the docks for an off-target bomb to land on it. Nan's needles clicked laboriously. Knitting was painful and difficult for her, with her finger-joints knobbly from arthritis, but, stubbornly, she carried on knitting – socks, pullovers, scarves, anything. If she carried on knitting, the arthritis hadn't won. And if she carried on knitting through air-raids, then Hitler hadn't won, either. She was so practised at it that she could knit in the dark. Rows and rows she knitted during air-raids.

After the raid there would be hot cocoa and then bed. Ronnie lay uncomfortably, wondering what he'd see if he could look straight through the roof of the shelter. Heinkels and Dorniers, maybe, in formation. That first afternoon, that sunny afternoon when he'd been coming back from the corner shop and seen dozens of bombers, wave after wave, it had been so exciting that he'd hardly thought of being frightened. Real Germans – the invasion everyone had been talking about! But there hadn't been an invasion, not yet. Now, mostly, they came at night. You could see them only as silhouettes against the sky, or sometimes pinned like a moth in the searchlights. And only if you were outside, where you weren't allowed to be.

Dad was outside. Or at least, dodging in and out from his warden's post – his job was to report on any damage done in his area, his square of streets, and to phone the fire and rescue services if they were needed. When the All Clear sounded he'd still be busy, checking up who was in the public shelters and whether anyone was missing.

"Should have stayed down in Devon, out of all this," Nan said sharply to Mum. "You and the kiddies."

"I'm not a kiddy!" Ronnie had said it so many times that he couldn't be bothered to say it again.

"Oh, Mum. How could I stand it down there, not knowing what was happening to you and Lennie?" Mum said. Lennie was Dad's name: Lennie Cooper. "Oh, it was nice though," she went on, "those two weeks in the country. Sea-views and fields instead of streets. Space and fresh air instead of everyone crammed together. Made the war seem such a long way off."

Ronnie lay there, listening. Nan must have

thought he was asleep, as she went on: "It's Ronnie I worry about. He'd be much better off out of this, down in Devon with his mates, with his teachers and proper school. He'll be getting himself into trouble before long."

Mum, cradling Patsy in her arms, said vaguely, "Oh, he's a good boy, really. He's bound to get up to mischief now and then. There there, Patsy-Pat. Don't you fret, Pat-a-Cake." She began humming softly, a nursery rhyme. Patsy, who was only two, had cried when the first bombs came but was now whimpering quietly, comforted by the rocking.

Engines droned, close overhead. Then the whine of a bomb dropping. Ronnie held his breath and bit his bottom lip – what would it be like to be alive and breathing one minute and then suddenly dead? Would you *know*? Then he heard the almost leisurely boom and spatter of high explosive, and knew that he was still alive. He pictured a house flung apart, tiles and plaster flying, a bath sticking out into space.

Someone's copped it, he thought, but not us. Not this time.

Much later, when the All Clear sounded and they were wearily trooping back indoors in the grey dawn light, Ronnie thought of the bomb-site boy. Where had he sheltered during the raid? Had he been safe in a shelter with his family? Was he, like Ronnie, going indoors for cocoa and bed?

There was something odd about that boy, Ronnie thought. The way he had appeared without a sound, then vanished in mid-conversation. Almost like a ghost.

But Ronnie didn't believe in ghosts. He yawned, and followed Nan into the kitchen.

* * * * *

Ronnie slept late in the morning. His bedroom was now Nan's; he had to sleep on a camp bed, wedged in between the dining-table and the fireplace. Mum, on her way out, and Dad, on his way in, must have come past him, but he'd slept through. His morning jobs were to fold up the camp bed and put it away in the outside store, stash his bedding under the sofa, then get Nan her tea and toast. It took Nan ages to get up and dressed in the morning; she moved about painfully, and fumbled at buttons with stiff fingers. Officially – according to Mum, that was – Ronnie was supposed to help her with fastenings and shoe-laces, but Nan fiercely resisted any such attempt: "Leave me be! I'll do it in my own time – I'm not helpless, not yet!"

Outside at last, Ronnie sniffed the air. You never knew what you'd see after an air-raid. Coronation Road was still intact, but the acrid smell of explosive hung in the air, laced with a warmer and more homely smell of horse-dung. Ronnie saw a neat pile in the road outside the corner-shop. If Dad were here, he'd go out with a shovel and bring it in for his garden. "Fresh horse manure! Nothing beats it."

And there was the horse himself – Lucky, the milkman's horse, clopping slowly along the street in the direction of his stable in Red Lion Yard. Ronnie waved, and Alf Deakins waved back from his box-seat at the front of the milk float. It made things seem normal, the milkman on his round. Ronnie didn't know how Alf did it, but every morning, raid or no raid, he collected his bottles from the depot and delivered them. Sometimes he had to make complicated detours to get past street barricades or roads strewn with rubble. Lucky, a stolid piebald, seemed unflustered by the changes of routine. In Devon, Ronnie had seen horses working the land, and a herd of cows coming in for milking. Odd to think that the very same cows, grazing their green shoulder of hillside, could have produced the milk Alf had just delivered to houses in the battered East End of London. Alf had cheap lodgings, a rented room in a house by the market; Ronnie wasn't sure exactly where, but he knew where Lucky lived. He had a stable in Red Lion Yard, off Gordon Street, behind a bombed-out pub.

"Did Jerry keep your dad busy last night, then?" Alf called.

"Not too bad, thanks." Dad usually came home at dawn, for breakfast and a snatch of sleep before putting in his hours at the sorting office. He'd had to get used to strange patterns of sleeping – in bed by early evening, up again at nine-thirty at night, to put on his makeshift ARP uniform and his tin helmet.

"'Op on, if you like," Alf offered. He sometimes gave Ronnie a ride back to the yard, where Ronnie cleaned out the horse's stable and helped groom and settle him. Alf usually rewarded him with a few pence, if he had any to spare.

But Ronnie shook his head. "Tomorrow, p'raps." He wanted, urgently, to go back to that bomb-site, to look for the boy. It was senseless, he knew – why should the boy be there, rather than anywhere else? But he had to check.

Alf raised a hand, and the piebald cob

plodded on, the reins slack on his rump. Alf could have fallen asleep if he liked – Lucky knew his own way home. According to Alf, he knew the whole milk round as well.

Ronnie cut through the market in Claypole Lane. Lots of the stallholders knew him; he sometimes helped Charlie Figgis unpack his fruit and veg in the morning, or with the clearing up at the end of the day. This time Ronnie only waved at Charlie, and pushed through the gap between the offal stall and the haberdasher's, aiming for Victoria Road beyond.

Then he saw him.

The boy. The bomb-site boy. Standing in a queue at a mobile canteen. His eyes were downcast; adults in front and behind him were talking over his head. His arms were folded tightly across his chest, hands tucked under his arms, as if he were chilled. It wasn't cold today, not for October. At the serving-hatch of the van, women in green uniform were handing out mugs of tea, and buns.

Ronnie went straight up to him. "Hey! You been bombed out?"

The boy's head jerked up. He stared at Ronnie, then recognised him. "Oh. Hello." He gave a thin little smile.

"What's wrong?"

"Nothing!" The boy's voice was hardly a whisper.

"Who're you with?" Ronnie glanced at the grown-ups in the queue. None of them seemed to be taking any notice of the boy. "Hardly got a wink," a sour-faced woman was saying, and someone else was complaining about the length of the queue.

"Shh! No one."

"Don't mind us! Push in, why don't you?" the sour-faced woman said, giving Ronnie a poke in the ribs. Without meaning to, he'd got into the queue. He felt in his pockets. He had a few pence, plenty for tea and a bun. He turned his back on the woman, who carried on moaning to the man next to her. The other boy seemed embarrassed by the attention. He stood with shoulders hunched, giving furtive glances at Ronnie.

"Where d'you live, then?" Ronnie asked, his voice barely more than a whisper.

The boy turned to him. He didn't speak, but his mouth framed the word: "Nowhere."

"What d'you mean?"

The boy leaned towards him. "Listen. I'll tell you, only not here, right?"

3 ✤ Dusty

With their mugs of tea and their rock buns, they sat side by side on the church steps.

"What d'you mean, you live nowhere?" Ronnie was impatient.

"Promise not to tell? Cross your heart and hope to die?"

Ronnie put down his mug and pointed his fingers in an X sign over his chest. "Cross my heart and hope to die."

The boy took a gulp of too-hot tea, swallowed quickly, then glanced around him and behind.

"I've run away. I'm on my own."

Ronnie was impressed. The boy looked frail, too slight and skinny to be a lone survivor.

"Who've you run away from, then?"

"My aunt. I was sent to live with her. She lives out in Woodford."

"So you came here, to the East End?" It didn't make sense to Ronnie. "It's safer out there. Here's where the bombs are."

The boy was devouring his rock bun like a starved dog, gulping it down. "Yes, I know," he said, through his next mouthful. "But it's easier to hide here. No one takes much notice. There are so many people."

"What was wrong with your aunt? And what's happened to your mum and dad?"

"She beat me, and shut me in her room. I hate her. I'd rather be on my own. My mum's dead and my dad – " The boy picked up a crumb from the ground, throwing it to a pigeon that had walked up close and was eyeing him. "He's in the RAF. He's a Spitfire pilot."

The pigeon gobbled the crumb and cocked its head, looking beadily at the two boys to see if there were more.

"Wow!" Ronnie said. "You mean he's a fighter pilot?"

The boy nodded.

Everyone knew what Prime Minister Churchill had said, back in August: "Never in the field of human conflict was so much owed by so many to so few." When Ronnie heard it on the radio, he had felt a swelling of pride, even though he didn't know anyone who flew Spitfires. When he was old enough – if the war was still on – he was going to be a Spitfire pilot.

It was nearly every boy's ambition – to be one of the flying aces who battled nightly against the German bombers, who sent Messerschmitts plummeting into the sea.

"He's not dead, is he?" Ronnie asked.

The boy shook his head vigorously. "No! He's one of the best – they never shot him down, but he got dozens of Germans. He's somewhere down in Sussex, still flying. I haven't seen him for ages."

Ronnie was silent for a few moments. He thought of his own father – short, stocky and bespectacled. Too short-sighted to fight in the last war, and now too old for this one. A Spitfire pilot for a dad would be something to be proud of. But the pilots he'd seen in the newspaper pictures were young men – hardly more than boys, really. They looked jaunty and brave, with their scarves slung round their necks and their caps at rakish angles. They were the Few, the elite. Heroes.

"How old is he then, your dad?" he asked. "I mean, most of those pilots aren't old enough to be dads."

The boy licked the last tiny crumbs of rock bun from the palm of his hand. "He's only twenty-nine. He got married young."

Ronnie's dad was over forty. Much too old. Yesterday, Ronnie had felt a kind of superiority, telling the boy about UXBs and bomb-sites. Now, he felt ashamed.

"What's your name, anyway?" he asked.

"Gerald," the boy said, making a wry face.

"Gerald! Jerry!" Ronnie seized on the name delightedly. "You're Jerry, you're German, the enemy!" He grasped an imaginary machine-gun and aimed it at the boy's chest. "Hur-hur-hur-hur-hur - "

"I knew you'd say that," the boy said sadly. "Everyone does. It was like that at school. Every time we played war games, they'd say: 'You're Jerry! You've got to be Jerry!' And that meant I always had to get killed. It's not fair! I didn't ask to be called Gerald."

He could have made up a different name, Ronnie thought – I'd have done.

"Haven't you got a middle name?" he asked.

"You could use that."

"That's even worse," the boy said glumly. "It's Eustace. That's my grandfather's name."

"Useless Eustace!" Ronnie joked.

The boy pulled a face. "No, thanks. What's your name?"

"Ronnie. Ronnie Cooper. I live a couple of

streets away, in Coronation Road. Look, I won't call you Jerry if you don't like it. What's your surname?"

"Miller."

"Dusty, then. Dusty Miller."

The boy looked puzzled. "Why?"

"Dusty Miller – you know. Haven't you heard that before? Everyone called Miller's called Dusty for a nickname. It's 'cos millers are always covered in flour dust."

"I didn't know. But I like Dusty. You can call me that. I like having a new name. It's like I'm someone different."

Gerald was quite a posh name, Ronnie thought. And Woodford was a lot posher than the East End – he'd been there once on a church picnic. It was on the edge of Epping Forest, and the houses were big, spaced well apart. It was Mum's dream to live out in Essex, away from the city. And now that he thought about it, Gerald was very well-spoken. Polite. The sort of boy Mum would like Ronnie to be friendly with, rather than Cheeky Chalky, as she called him. Gerald – Dusty – didn't seem the sort of boy to know his way around West Ham.

"Where do you live? What do you eat?" Ronnie asked.

"You won't tell anyone?"

"No, but – " Ronnie was unsure. "Shouldn't someone know – someone who could help you? My mum – she's in the WVS, she'd know what to do – "

"No!" Dusty stood up. "If you tell anyone, they'll make me go back to my aunt's! I won't go! Besides, you've promised! You can't go back on it now. I'm not telling you any more unless you promise to keep it secret!"

"All right! I promise!" Ronnie said hastily. He reached into his pocket and pulled out a threepenny-bit, along with some bits of fluff and a bottle-top. "Look, d'you want another bun?"

"Yes, please." Dusty's eyes brightened.

"Then you tell me everything, right? You wait here and I'll bring them over."

While he waited in the queue with the coin hot in his hand, Ronnie kept looking across to Dusty on the steps. In an odd way, he felt responsible. To him, the boy looked conspicuous, out-of-place, but all the adults around were too busy with their own concerns to take any notice of him. Someone was talking in a hushed voice about where you could get black-market bacon; someone else was anxious about a sister in Bermondsey. No one apart from

Ronnie so much as looked in Dusty's direction.

"It's easy, really," Dusty explained, eating his second bun. "There are so many places to hide. Cellars, bombed-out houses. You can find food in cupboards, tins, blankets, whatever you need. Like that place the other day."

"You sleep there?"

Dusty nodded. "Then, when there's been a raid, there's always mobile canteens, and rest centres. I just join in with whoever's going there. You don't have to pay, not straight after a raid. If anyone asks who I'm with I just say my mum's on her way, then I slip away again. It always works."

"But – " Ronnie thought of his dad, who was responsible for knowing where everyone slept, in case of raids. "What if you're in a bombed-out house and it gets hit again? No one'd know you were there!"

Dusty shrugged. "I can go in the shelters, like everyone else. Or down the Underground."

"You've been down there?"

"There are so many people, no one asks questions."

"But what about when it's winter? You can't sleep in house ruins then."

"Look, you've never met my aunt. You don't

know how horrible she is." Dusty finished the bun and rubbed the palms of his hands on his shorts. "Anyway, what shall we do now? Haven't you got friends?"

"They're all in Devon," Ronnie said. "I spend most of the time on my own. I'll show you some of my special places, if you like."

4 ✤ Red Lion Yard

When Chalky had been here, a favourite game had been trying to race the Woolwich ferry. One of them would go across the Thames on the paddle-steamer, while the other would race through the tunnel and try to beat it; then they'd swap for the journey back. Ronnie had once cannoned into a cross businessman in mid-tunnel. They were both winded, gasping for air, but the man had hooked Ronnie's sweater with the crook of his umbrella and pulled him in like a fish while he got enough breath back to deliver a harsh telling-off.

Leading the way through the market and down Spicer's Alley, Ronnie told Dusty about it, acting the part of the red-faced man.

"Let's do that! Go on, can we?" Dusty asked.

"If you want. After we've seen Alf."

They'd already been to the chestnut tree in the park, searching for ripe conkers; then to the corner shop in Mill Street, where nice old Mr Tomlin gave them broken biscuits in exchange for sweeping up the floor. "You don't want to get in with this one," Mr Tomlin had told Dusty, with his smile that gave him two chins. "More trouble than a barrel of monkeys, he is. If there's trouble, he'll find it, Ronnie will." But he was only joking, and when they left he said they could come back tomorrow and help tidy his store-room.

Ronnie remembered that he was supposed to be seeing his tutor this afternoon. Perhaps, if he stopped thinking about it, it would slip from his memory altogether.

The row of shops in Gordon Street had been bombed three nights ago, but some of them were still, defiantly, doing business. 'More Open Than Usual,' was painted in red splashy letters on a board propped by a greengrocer's whose whole frontage had gone. Rubble and glass had been swept into a neat pile on the pavement, and the greengrocer had simply used the extra space to display his carrots, cabbages, beans and potatoes, propping the crates on trestles, as on a market stall. Through what had once been the inside wall of the shop, you could see right through to the greengrocer's private room – the fireplace, grandfather clock, and a cat dozing in an armchair.

The Red Lion had once been a coaching inn, with a big stableyard behind. Now the pub was in ruins, having taken a direct hit in one of the first air-raids. Someone had taken away the painted signboard – a rampant red lion on a black background.

"The landlord and his wife were killed," Ronnie said, matter-of-factly. He hadn't known them. "The missus, she was blown right out into the street. Not a mark on her. It was the blast killed her."

"That's awful!" Dusty said, staring wide-eyed into the collapsed building. It was like all the others – wallpaper shredded and tattered, bits of furniture and crockery all covered in dust, part of a flight of stairs leading nowhere. What had been the bar was strewn with wooden chair spars and shards of painted mirror, and an enamelled advert for Virginia Flake.

Incongruously, a picture still hung askew on its nail on a fragment of wall half-way up to what had been the first floor. It was an old-fashioned print of a horse and rider – Ronnie could see that, even through its cracked and dusty glass.

Ronnie pointed to it. "If it was easier to get to I'd climb up for that, only look at those stairs.

The whole lot'd come down."

"There must be a cellar," Dusty said. "Pubs always have one, don't they, for the crates of beer, and kegs and stuff?"

Ronnie looked at him. "You thinking of moving house? Fancy having beer on tap?"

"I don't like beer," Dusty said quite seriously.

Ronnie led the way round the back. The inn had a small garden, with Michaelmas daisies straggling over the uncut grass, and a tree with orange berries. What had once been the stableyard formed three sides of a square. Most of the stables had been turned into garages or lock-up sheds for small businesses – Alf's horse Lucky lived in one of two remaining stables at the farthest corner from the inn. They were old-fashioned, leading off an interior corridor, with bars at the windows and cobbled floors – very grand, Alf said, for a milkman's horse. "And one that looks like he oughta be pulling a gypsy caravan, at that."

The horse's striped face lifted to the window bars and he gave a breathy whicker of greeting as they approached. Ronnie unbolted the stable door and went in. Dusty went straight to the horse and leaned his face against his neck, patting him. Lucky nuzzled his shoulder in return.

"I help look after him," Ronnie said importantly, "and sometimes Alf even lets me take the reins."

"He smells lovely," Dusty said. "Like the country. Do you ever ride him?"

There was a movement from the adjoining stable. Dusty ducked under the horse's neck in alarm, as Alf rose from the straw-stack and looked at the boys blearily. He had been sleeping there, huddled in his overcoat.

"It's only Alf," Ronnie said, as Dusty showed signs of bolting from the stable. "He's all right."

"Who's this?" Alf said, then gave a massive yawn, showing several missing teeth.

"It's Dusty," Ronnie said. "He's my friend."

"Dusty, eh?" Alf clambered stiffly down, then came round to Lucky's stable. He extended a weathered hand to Dusty. "Dusty Miller, eh?"

"Yes." Dusty looked startled; he backed away as if he thought Alf might grab him. "How do you know?"

"Dusty Miller! See, I told you!" Ronnie said.

Alf's hand was still held out. Dusty glanced at Ronnie for reassurance, then shook hands briefly.

"Pleased to make your acquaintance, I'm sure," Alf said.

"How do you do, Mr – " Dusty said, with his nice-boy manners. "I'm very sorry to have woken you up."

Alf laughed, brushing straw off his threadbare coat. "Alf. Just call me Alf. 'S all right. I usually get a bit of shut-eye around now, what with having to get up so early."

According to Mrs Huggins next door to Ronnie, Alf had been in the habit of drinking every evening in the Red Lion, sitting there till closing time, making a couple of half-pints last all evening. After that, he did a bit of fire-watching till it was time to harness up Lucky and go round to the depot for the milk. He had no family – only Lucky. Ronnie didn't know where he went now that the pub was in ruins, but guessed that he'd found an alternative. There were lots of other pubs.

"He's a lovely horse, Mr – Alf." Dusty had gone back to Lucky, and was stroking his neck, smoothing his rough mane. "Aren't you afraid to keep him here though, with the bombing raids?"

Alf gave his wheezy laugh that sounded more like coughing. "He'll be right as rain. Bin hit once, ent it, the Red Lion? They say lightning never strikes the same place twice." He slapped the horse's neck, his tired old eyes brightening with pride. "You're a good-un, aincha, me ole boy? Anyway," he added, turning to the boys, "his name's Lucky. That's got to mean something, ennit?"

* * * * *

"Tell me more about your dad. About him shooting down Jerries."

They were eating again – penny doughnuts bought from the baker's on the corner. They sat on crates out in the yard, while Alf, making the most of his spare hours, snored gently from the spare stable. You got a good open view of sky from here. The barrage balloons bobbed and swayed gently on their tethers like great airborne fish; much higher up was the vapour-trail of an aircraft. Ours or theirs? Ronnie wondered.

"Hey, look up there! Can you see if it's a Spit? That could be him!" He pointed with a sugary wedge of doughnut.

"Who?"

"Your dad. Weren't you listening?"

"Oh. Yes," Dusty said vaguely.

"D'you think it is? Does he fly over London? Or is he down at the White Cliffs of Dover, intercepting them as they come in over the Channel?"

"Don't know."

Ronnie couldn't understand Dusty's hesitation. If his dad had flown Spitfires, he wouldn't have needed any prompting.

"What was the bravest thing he ever did?" Ronnie stuffed the last doughy piece into his mouth.

"Oh, loads of things," Dusty said airily.

"Go on, then – tell me one!"

"All right." Dusty sat up straight, cross-legged.

"He was over at Dunkirk, protecting the troops. He shot down one of those Stuka dive-bombers. Then three Messerschmitts chased him away across the Channel. He was on his own, haring for home. He could have cleared off and left them standing, but he wasn't going to miss the chance of another kill. He checked his altitude and gained height, then swung round so the sun was behind him. Then he came up behind the formation and went straight for the middle one. Da-da-da-da-da-" He mimed, contorting his face. "It was on fire, the middle one. He saw it go right down into the sea, blazing. Then the second – "

"He didn't get all three?"

"No. The second one was damaged – he saw it turn back for the coast, flying low. Now there was just the third. He went for it, guns blazing. He saw the black holes ripped in the fuselage.

Then he saw the Jerry bail out. He jumped from the cockpit and his parachute opened. And the Messerschmitt went on low, like this – " He held out a flattened hand – "till it was skimming the waves. And then it hit, and somersaulted, and broke up into bits. All Dad saw was the oil floating on the water. But he didn't see any more, 'cos he had to get back while he still had fuel."

"Wow! He must be incredibly brave."

Dusty's chin jutted; his face took on an obstinate expression.

"Course he is. Stands to reason. You can't be a Spitfire pilot without being brave."

"If it'd been me I'd have shot the pilot too. While he was coming down by parachute."

Dusty looked at him. "No, you wouldn't. I bet you wouldn't."

"Would!"

"Wouldn't!"

"Would!"

Ronnie was the first to start pushing. Dusty, overbalancing, righted himself and pushed back. To Ronnie it was just a game, but Dusty, obviously not much of a fighter, wriggled away and scrambled to his feet, his face tight with fear.

"Go on! Fight like your dad!" Ronnie jeered.

Dusty stepped back. "What d'you mean?"

Ronnie was amazed to see tears welling in the other boy's eyes. With another feeble shove, Dusty turned and ran out of the yard.

"Hey, come back! I was only messing about!" Ronnie followed him as far as the pub. Dusty, thinner and lighter, was surprisingly quick on his feet. Also, Ronnie remembered, he was expert at hiding. There was no sign of him.

It was a stupid way to end the afternoon. Ronnie looked in a few shop doorways and down alleys, then gave up and walked slowly back home. Only as he pushed open the front door did he remember that he should have been at his lesson.

* * * * *

Mum hadn't forgotten. She came zooming in on him like the Messerschmitt had zoomed in on Dusty's dad.

"Ronnie Cooper! I don't know how you've got the nerve to come strolling back in, calm as ninepence! I've had your tutor round here this afternoon. And let me tell you I wasn't very pleased to hear what he had to say!"

"Oh." Ronnie stood on the doormat.

"You might well Oh." Mum barred his way, hands on hips. "You'll Oh all right when I've finished with you, young man. You're not leaving the house tomorrow, not for five minutes, till it's time for your lesson at half-past two. And you'll be there smart and punctual and ready to learn!"

She made him go up to his room – Nan's room, as it was now – with his school-books, and no tea. He had to study till bedtime, she said, to make up for the missed lessons.

Later, while she was busy putting Patsy to bed, Nan came up.

"I've come to check you're blacked-out properly up here, all right?" she said.

Then she took out her hand from under her apron and gave him a slice of bread-and-dripping. She was a good'un, Nan was.

5 ✤ The Corner Shop Bomb

Ronnie couldn't sleep. Never had the slatted bench in the Anderson seemed less comfortable, or his blankets more itchy. Even the click of Nan's knitting needles – usually a homely, comforting sound – was irritating. He shifted, turned to face the corrugated wall, turned back again. Mum was sewing, in the pool of light from the Hurricane lamp. She stooped to thread her needle, snipped a thread, then carried on with quick, neat stitches, darning one of Dad's socks. Her voice and Nan's rose and fell, rose and fell, as they chattered on about nothing much, the way grown-ups did.

Ronnie couldn't stop thinking about Dusty. Where was he now? Huddled in a ruin somewhere, cold and shivering and alone? Ronnie wouldn't like that. Although he wouldn't confess it to Dusty, not to anyone, he knew he'd be scared, all on his own with an air-raid coming.

He doesn't know what to do, Ronnie thought. He's a posh boy from Woodford; he doesn't know how to look after himself. When a bomb comes, you have to open your mouth wide – the blast can burst your eardrums if your mouth's tight shut. Does Dusty know that? I should have told him.

He thought: I bet I'll never see him again. P'raps he's gone back to Woodford, to his aunt. It wasn't my fault, anyway. I didn't chase him away. He ran. No one's going to put the blame on me.

And then the air overhead was torn apart, with a sound like giant sheets ripping, followed by a slower, deep boom. Ronnie remembered to open his mouth wide as a shock wave hit the shelter. Mum grabbed his leg as if she thought he might hurtle through the ceiling if she didn't hold him down. Patsy started to cry. Debris spattered like hailstones; Ronnie could hear and feel it, even through the foot-deep earth that covered the roof.

But they were still alive. They looked at each other. Mum passed the sobbing Patsy over to Nan, then pushed aside the tarpaulin curtain and ventured outside, shining the dim beam of her torch at the ground. The acrid smell of high explosive was everywhere, in the shelter, in the air outside. Ronnie felt himself trembling, and tried to clench his muscles to make himself stop.

He thought: a real hero, like Dusty's dad, wouldn't tremble. He's used to facing danger without flinching. All I've got to do is sit in a shelter.

"Close," Nan said, "but not that close. Didn't have our names on it, that one."

But did it have Dad's name on it? Or Dusty's? Ronnie didn't want to think. It was so close to the houses, it must have had someone's. It was no use thinking it had hit the docks or the railway, this time. And perhaps, at this very moment in some German factory, someone was inscribing the name Ronnie Cooper on tomorrow night's bomb.

Mum came back. "Can't see anything. Not our house, nor the neighbours. Must have been close, though. I'll go out as soon as the All Clear sounds."

* * * * *

Morning was surprisingly normal, at first. Mum went out early, taking Patsy with her; Dad sent a message round to say that he hadn't been hurt but was busy with the rescue services. Where, he didn't say. Three of the windows on the front of the house had been blown out, and Mum had stuck cardboard over the gaps, with brown sticky tape.

"Don't forget, you're to stay indoors till quarter to two," she had warned Ronnie. "Clearing up the garden can wait till later. I'll be back at twelve and I expect to see you at the table with your school-books."

But Ronnie couldn't concentrate on his sums and his grammar, not till he'd looked for Dusty. It needn't take long, just a quick dash –

"And where are you off to, Sunny Jim?" It was Nan, coming slowly down the stairs. One gnarled hand gripped the banister rail. Of all days, she had to come down early today!

"Oh – " Ronnie was caught with a hand on the door-knob. "I – I just had to go out and see someone. Not for long."

"I see. And who might that be?" Nan came down the last two stairs, arriving on the landing-strip of carpet with a thud of triumph.

"Just someone. A friend."

Nan eyed him beadily. "Secret, is it?"

"Yes," Ronnie mumbled.

"Between you and who?"

"I can't tell you, Nan – I promised!"

"All right." Nan fumbled in her pocket. "How about I make it legal, then – you go and fetch my pills for me, I won't say a word about wherever else you might decide to go? As long as you're quick, mind, and don't get up to anything you shouldn't. I don't want to get in trouble with your mum, any more than you do."

"Thanks, Nan!" Ronnie took the piece of paper. "I'll do the toast soon as I get back, all right?"

"I can do toast." Nan's voice wafted back as she headed for the kitchen. "I'm not so senile that I can't cope with a bit of toast."

Ronnie closed the front door behind him and set off at a run for the chemist's. Then, turning the corner of Mill Street towards the small parade of shops, he stopped dead. The chemist's wasn't there. Mr Tomlin's corner shop wasn't there. He saw barricades, rubble, the side of a house torn clean off, gaping open, with pipe-ends sticking out like torn blood-vessels. There were men digging, heaving at brickwork and beams; there was an ambulance. As Ronnie stood in shock, he saw a human shape covered in a sheet by the roadside.

"Poor old Mr Tomlin." Two neighbours from Ronnie's street were standing by the crossing.

"Mrs T. and all, I heard," said Mrs Fellows. "It won't be the same without the old corner shop."

"Is there someone else in there?" Mrs March

nodded towards the rescue team.

"The old mother-in-law, Alf Deakins told me."

"Terrible shame," tutted Mrs Fellows. "I was talking to Mrs T. only yesterday. I suppose we'll have to walk all the way to the High Street, now," she grumbled.

Kind old Mr Tomlin, with his face that creased into smiles, and his jokes! And Mrs Tomlin who was always limping on her bad leg, stumping heavily around the shop, grunting when she had to reach up to a top shelf. Her bad leg wouldn't bother her any more. Ronnie thought of the shop floor he had swept only yesterday, and Mr Tomlin's store-room that would stay forever untidied. What was the point of it all – sweeping up, tidying up, the shops trying to stay open? You might as well pick stones out of the path of an avalanche.

Ronnie thought - one day, we'll come out of our shelter and find there's nothing left. Everything will have been smashed to bits. All of the East End, all of London. Just stones and rubble and burst water pipes. And we'll be in the middle of it, like rats.

It might be better to be killed. At least then you wouldn't know ...

He ran on ahead of the two women towards the High Street, where there was another chemist, but he couldn't stop thinking about what he had seen. There was a sort of horrible thrill to the suddenness of it – the randomness of where the bomb struck, like a finger jabbing from the sky. You – no, you, and you. Your turn tonight. Mr Tomlin, alive and joking yesterday, lay cold on a stretcher with his face covered. Who next?

Dusty. What if – ?

Suddenly the new name seemed horribly appropriate. Ronnie pictured Dusty lying half-buried by masonry, his mouth and eyes clogged by dust. No one would know.

Only Ronnie.

6 ✣ In the Fireplace

He ran and ran, till the stitch in his side was like a blunt knife sawing through him. Past barricades and shut-off streets, an abandoned car, a lamp-post that had been knocked askew and pulled up part of the pavement with it. He smelled gas and sewage; his feet crunched glass. Hurtling round a corner, he collided splat with a propped-up board that said 'Open as Usual', turned as it skidded face-up into the road, then regained his balance and ran on.

"Oi!" yelled the shopkeeper. Ronnie glimpsed him, a sad figure in the remains of his drapery shop, but there was no time to turn back. He accelerated, swerving round a woman with a pram.

Victoria Terrace. The bombed-out house now wore a neglected look – no rescue teams in attendance, no one picking through the debris. Ronnie clambered over the toppled garden wall, swung his leg over a window-sill that had no window, and was inside.

"Dusty!" he yelled. "Dusty, you there?"

No answer. He looked, room by room, then out in the garden, even in the Anderson shelter. Not a sign. Not even a fresh footprint on the flattened earth of the vegetable plot. He turned back to what had been the main room.

"Dusty!" he called again. His own voice bounced back at him, mocking.

Then he saw it. His eyes widened.

In front of the fireplace, slicing through carpet and floorboards. A grey torpedo shape, sleek and finned, with its nose buried in the floor.

* * * * *

A bomb.

Ronnie froze. His mouth opened silently. He'd been stomping and clambering about, inches from an unexploded bomb! He risked a look upwards. There was no other damage; there was no roof left for it to smash through. He looked again at the fireplace. The bomb was still there – for a mind-fuddled second he hoped he'd only imagined it.

It might be a dud. Or it might not.

Next to it, on the floor, was the toy horse Dusty had thrown away, the first time they'd met. He must get out. Tell someone. He gave a small, experimental cough. He moved a hand. He placed one foot very carefully behind him, then the other, walking backwards, turning his head so that he didn't crash over debris. Slowly, hardly daring to breathe, he turned his body. His neck prickled; the bomb might take its chance to explode, now he'd turned his back on it. Very carefully he lifted one leg over the window-sill, then the other. He turned to make sure the bomb really was there, then stealthily, as in a game of Grandmother's Footsteps, sneaked out of the front garden and on to the pavement.

He looked around wildly. There was no one in sight – no policeman or warden. The adjoining house was boarded up, but the one two doors along looked inhabited. For UXBs, whole streets had to be evacuated – yet there must be people in there, getting their breakfast, discussing last night's raid, unaware that a stray, lethal bomb was poised within yards of them. What if the split boards that were supporting it gave way? What if it toppled over sideways and crashed to the floor?

Ronnie bounded up the steps and knocked on the door. He banged again, frantically. A woman in a flowered apron opened it, and looked at Ronnie with suspicion. "What is it?"

"There's a bomb," Ronnie gasped, "in the ruined house, two doors down. Have you got a phone?"

She frowned. She was the sort of woman who didn't like kids, he could tell. "Is this your idea of a game, young man?"

"No! You've got to believe me! Come and see for yourself – no, don't, it's not safe – "

The woman's expression wavered, annoyance giving way to doubt. "You saw it?"

"Yes! I nearly fell over it! You've got to phone someone, and quick – the warden, the bomb disposal – it might go off any second – "

A hand shot out and grabbed the back of his shirt collar. "You come with me. I'll want your name and address."

Her grip was firm. Protesting, Ronnie was dragged into a room crammed with furniture – little tables, padded armchairs, a piano, with framed photographs cluttering every surface. "Wait there," the woman ordered, wedging him between the piano and a card-table. You'd think he'd done something shameful, instead of trying to save her life! But at least this house had a telephone, and the woman knew which number to ask for.

"Apparently there's an unexploded bomb, two doors down." She spoke as calmly as someone reporting a minor nuisance, like boys stealing milk-bottles. "That's right. Last night, I imagine. The name's Warren, 5 Victoria Terrace, and the boy who found it is – "

"Larry Green," Ronnie improvised.

"Larry Green," the woman repeated. "Yes, he'll wait with me."

Oh no he wouldn't! Now that he knew the call had been made, and help was on its way, he'd finished here. He darted into the hallway.

"Wait, you little monkey!"

But he was out of the front door, slamming it behind him. He leaped down the steps and ran out to the street.

* * * * *

At the High Street he slowed, panting, remembering why he'd come out. Nan's pills! He shoved a hand into his shorts pocket. The piece of paper was still there, crumpled up, and he was supposed to be indoors doing his sums. But even Mum couldn't really object to his disobedience, now that he'd saved people's lives!

The odd thing was that he didn't feel like a hero, not at all. And that woman certainly hadn't treated him as one. You'd have thought he'd put the bomb there, the way she'd gone on. And Dusty! He still hadn't found Dusty. He'd try the Underground next. But first, he'd get Nan's pills and take them home. She'd let him go out again; she could usually be relied on to take his side.

Ten minutes later, with the pill-bottle clutched in his hand, he walked up his own front path. He reached out his hand with the key, then stepped back in alarm as the door was flung open.

"Ronald Cooper!" It was Mum, looking far from pleased. "I told you at least five times you had to stay indoors – wasn't that enough for you to understand?"

She shouldn't have been here – she was supposed to be safely out of the way, at the rest centre!

"But – " Ronnie waved the bottle of pills, his alibi.

Mum didn't even glance at it. For the second time that morning, Ronnie found himself hauled through a front door. Mum's grip on his arm was like a steel clamp.

"But nothing! I've heard enough of your excuses. Get in here."

7 ✤ Runaway

There was someone else in the front room with Mum and Nan. A slim, neat woman in a green suit sat at the table. She had wire spectacles, and hair pulled back into a bun, and wore her gas-mask in its box slung across her shoulder, very correct. They were having tea, and squashed-fly biscuits. She must be a special visitor; biscuits used up a lot of the sugar ration.

"Here he is at last," Mum said. "Tuck your shirt in, Ronald, and make yourself respectable. This is Miss Flitwick-Price. She's an Evacuation Officer."

"Hello, Ronald." Miss Flitwick-Price put down her cup and saucer, stood up and shook hands with him, as if he were grown-up.

"It's Ronnie," he said. Mum only called him Ronald when she was annoyed.

"Right you are, Ronnie, then," said Miss Flitwick-Price, and smiled. Magnified by the lenses of her glasses, her eyes were big and green, matching her suit. She wasn't really as old as the bun and the suit made her look at first glance. She was a lot younger than Mum, anyway.

Ronnie glanced from her face to Mum's and then to Nan's. Nan gave a wry half-smile from her armchair in the corner, her knitting needles clacking away. That showed she was anxious. Evacuation Officer, Ronnie thought? What's going on here? Am I going to be packed off to Devon again?

"It's lucky I was here – I'd normally be at the rest centre, the one in Victoria Road," Mum explained to the visitor. "I popped back because Patsy wet herself! – that's my two-year-old – and I needed to pick up some clean knickers. Now tell Miss Flitwick-Price what she wants to know, Ronnie, there's a good boy." Her voice was much friendlier now. She didn't want Miss Flitty-Whatnot to know how angry she was, he could tell.

"Sit down, Ronnie," the young woman said. "I think you can help me. I'm looking for a boy called Gerald Miller. Have you seen him?"

Ronnie opened his mouth, closed it again, looked at Nan, and knew he'd given himself away before he said a word. He'd had enough practice at telling fibs – he ought to be better at it! He sat down awkwardly at the table, beside his mother.

"Tell the truth, Ronald," his mother said.

"Apparently someone saw you with this boy yesterday. It's no use pretending."

"I did see him," Ronnie said. "Yesterday. And the day before. But I don't know where he is now." That was true enough, anyway.

"What did he tell you?" Miss Flitwick-Price leaned forward urgently. "About where he's staying, where he spends the nights?"

"I don't know. He told me he ran away from his aunt in Woodford. That's all I know."

"Aunt in Woodford?" Miss Flitwick-Price shook her head. "Is that what he told you?"

"Isn't that the truth?" said Mum.

"No." The young woman looked at Ronnie. "I was just about to explain, Ronnie, when you came in. This boy's been missing for nearly a fortnight now. He may well have an aunt in Woodford, but his home's in Leytonstone. He was evacuated to Somerset with his school, billeted with a nice family – there was a son his own age. But he ran away. Climbed out of his bedroom window one night, and disappeared."

"Why? Was he unhappy?" Nan asked.

Miss Flitwick-Price screwed round in her chair to look at her. "Not with his billet, no. They were a very kindly couple, Mr and Mrs Medway – most concerned when the boy vanished. Had the whole village out searching, and contacted me straight away."

"Homesick, I suppose," Mum said, pouring more tea. "I know how he felt. I was in Devon, you know – we all were, the four of us – that's me and Ronnie and little Patsy. My husband's an ARP warden, you know. But I hated the thought of the family being split up."

Ronnie fidgeted his feet under the table. Why wouldn't she keep quiet? If only she'd stop nattering, he'd hear about Dusty.

"It wasn't homesickness with Gerald," Miss Flitwick-Price said. "He had bad news about his father."

"His father? The Spitfire pilot?" Ronnie burst out. "He couldn't have been killed, or anything – not two weeks ago! Dusty – I mean Gerald – told me about him yesterday!"

"Spitfire pilot?" Miss Flitwick-Price shook her head. "No. That was the boy's fantasy, I imagine. The truth is a lot less glamorous."

Ronnie stared. Nan's needles stopped clicking; she rolled up her knitting on her lap and leaned forward to listen.

"The boy's father was an RAF pilot, yes," the young woman continued. "But in Bomber Command, not fighters. He'd had previous flying experience so he was one of the first to volunteer – as soon as war looked likely. He flew on operations for almost a year. Then he lost his nerve. Quite suddenly. Couldn't get back into his plane. He quite simply refused. When members of his crew reasoned with him, he had a shaking fit, then burst into tears, then threatened anyone who came near him."

"Poor man!" Nan said.

Miss Flitwick-Price glanced at her. "The RAF doesn't look at it that way, unfortunately. Anyone who loses his nerve is branded LMF. That stands for Lack of Moral Fibre. He was taken away, and stripped of his rank – his pilot's wings ripped off his jacket. He'll spend the rest of the war sweeping out huts."

Ronnie looked down at the tablecloth. He prised dirt from under his thumbnail. This was Dusty's father, the hero! Far from picking Jerry planes out of the sky, he didn't even have the nerve to get into his own. Real heroes didn't have shaking fits or burst into tears. Stripped of his pilot's wings! There could be nothing more shameful.

And Dusty! What a little liar! Just wait till I see him, Ronnie thought – if I ever do –

Nan shoved her knitting to the floor. "That's atrocious!" she hissed.

"Mrs Miller wrote to Gerald, explaining that his father was on enforced leave and was coming to visit him," Miss Flitwick-Price continued, "but Gerald took it very badly, it seems. Ran away to avoid seeing him. Mr and Mrs Medway found the letter still on his bed."

"It's disgraceful!" Nan snapped.

"A disgrace for the family, certainly. I expect the father wanted to see the boy himself, to explain."

"I don't mean the disgrace for the family!" Nan rose stiffly to her feet. "I mean the disgraceful way the RAF treats these people! Haven't we learned anything from the last war?"

"Sit down, Mum," Ronnie's mother soothed.

"No! I won't sit down!" Nan seemed about to move towards the door, but she waved a hand, impatient with her stiff limbs, her slowness. "Ronnie, go and fetch my photo, will you? The one on the dressing-table."

Glad to escape from the fraught atmosphere, Ronnie dashed up to his old bedroom. It smelled old-ladyish now, the air full of lavender and embrocation. There was only one photograph, framed in a heavy stand – of Nan's husband, long dead. Ronnie knew him only from Nan's old photos, some of them sepia-coloured and faded with age. In this one, Grandad was a young soldier in uniform, grinning.

He took the photo down and handed it to Nan. She was sitting, but very upright and stern, her cheeks flushed with indignation. She took the photograph from Ronnie and held it up for Miss Flitwick-Price to see.

"My husband. Fought in the last lot, the Great War. The Somme and Third Ypres. Not a hero, not specially – not as far as the military was concerned. Just an ordinary soldier."

"I'm very sorry," Miss Flitwick-Price said. "He was killed, was he?"

"No, he wasn't killed. Not in the war," Nan said. "But he never forgot it. That's my point. It stayed with him always. He'd wake up, shouting – years after the war, right up till he died, when this one – " Nan nodded at Ronnie – "was just a baby. My Jack was still there, in some stinking hell-hole. Yelling out to a wounded mate – trying to crawl out into no-man's-land, to bring him back in. 'I'm coming, Charlie, I'm coming,' he'd shout. Nearly every night he tried to rescue this Charlie. He'd be yelling, shaking, sweating – yes, even crying," she added defiantly. "He was in no-man's-land for the rest of his life. That's what war does." She put the photograph down.

"Not a hero, not particularly," she added. "Just an ordinary soldier. Just an ordinary man who'd seen too many terrible things." She looked at Miss Flitwick-Price. "Lack of Moral Fibre, eh? That's what they call it these days, is it, when a man can't take any more? That boy's poor father flew on operations for a whole year, but that counts for nothing! As soon as he shows signs of nerves, he's a piece of useless equipment, fit for nothing but the scrap heap!"

Anyone would have thought Miss Flitwick-Price was personally responsible for denouncing Dusty's father as a coward.

"All right, Mum," Ronnie's mother said, embarrassed by the outburst. "I'll make us all another cup of tea, shall I?"

"Yes, thank you," Miss Flitwick-Price said. "I'm very sorry about your husband, Mrs - "

"Lumsden," Nan said. She picked up her knitting.

" – but I must ask Ronnie some more questions. We've established that Gerald was in this area, but we're no closer to knowing where he actually is now."

* * * * *

There was no chance of skipping his lesson today – Mum escorted him round to the church hall herself. She led him right inside and plonked him down at his makeshift desk. "There!" she said to the surprised tutor. "No chance of this skallywag truanting again! And extra homework for tonight, if you don't mind, Mr Hegley. I want this young man kept out of mischief. He can make up everything he's missed."

Mr Hegley gave him a sideways look. "Ah, how nice to see you, Ronnie! It's good of you to drop in. I hope it hasn't interfered with more urgent plans?"

Ronnie scowled. They were enjoying it, the pair of them – showing him up in front of the class. Mr Hegley was a youngish man, unfit for military service – he was thin, pale and hollow-chested. All right for him, Ronnie thought, to sit here bossing people about – he didn't have to face any tougher sort of life in the army or air-force.

By the time Ronnie got home, he'd forgotten all about being a hero, finding the unexploded bomb. Dad, home for tea, had heard about it. He was sitting with his elbows on the table while he ate. Ronnie always got told off for that.

"D'you know, some young lad reported a UXB today! Name of Larry Green – no one you know, I suppose?"

"No," Ronnie said.

"Doesn't it go to prove what I've always told you? It's dangerous playing on bomb-sites! There it was, this bomb, wedged in a fireplace, and this idiotic lad clambering about within inches of it! Could have got himself blown to smithereens!"

"But at least he found it!" Ronnie was indignant. "No one knew it was there, otherwise!"

"Well, yes. Bomb disposal got to it. Had to move everyone out of the nearby houses for the afternoon, but they're all back now."

So the bomb hadn't gone off. Ronnie didn't know whether to be relieved or disappointed. There was no point revealing himself as Larry Green – that would be asking for a larruping. Dad slurped his tea, then waved a piece of Eccles cake at Ronnie. "So my point is, young feller-me-lad, you stay well clear of trouble! There's enough danger on the streets, without you going looking for it. I don't want to be picking up the pieces next time there's a bomb!"

Picking up the pieces was exactly what Dad did, every night, helping the rescue services. Ronnie looked at him. Dad looked tired. And old. His hair was thinning – he was a small, bespectacled gnome of a man. Ronnie was already as tall as him.

Ronnie thought of the lean, grinning Spitfire pilot he'd like to have for a father, the hero of the skies – the father Dusty had described. But Dusty's father wasn't really like that, either.

* * * * *

Two hours later, Ronnie stood by Nan's bedroom window, looking out at the darkening sky. The window, like all the others in the house, was criss-crossed with brown sticky-tape. It was probably the tape that held the glass in place, after last night's blast.

Today seemed to have gone on for ever, he thought gloomily. He was supposed to be doing his extra homework – Mum had moved all Nan's lavender bottles and pills and stuff off the dressing-table so that he could sit there, facing his reflection in the three-sided mirror – but he couldn't concentrate at all. There was one thing he hadn't done today, and that was find Dusty.

All these other things – the bomb, and Miss Hat-trick Splice, and the lesson, had got in the way. He wasn't going to see Dusty again, he was sure. Especially if Dusty knew about Miss F-P chasing him. He'd have made himself scarce.

Into Ronnie's mind slid the picture of the

chipped toy horse, lying on the floor of the ruined house near the bomb. He thought of Dusty holding it in his hand, looking at it, then chucking it aside.

Lucky. The milkman's horse. The warm stable. That's where Dusty would be. Why hadn't he thought of it before?

He moved towards the door, then stopped to think. He wouldn't be allowed out of the house, not now. Only if he said he knew where Gerald Miller was, and that would mean breaking his promise. He'd been forced, earlier today, to reveal that he and Dusty had first met in a ruined house – that's why Mum and Dad were both being so sharp with him.

He'd have to get out of the house secretly. But Mum, Dad, Nan and Patsy were all downstairs, and the door to the hall was open – he could hear the radio. They didn't trust him to stay where he'd been put.

He went back to the window and looked down at the tiled roof of the lavatory, which was a small lean-to built against the back of the house.

Dusty had climbed out of his bedroom window, to escape. Miss Flitwick-Price had said so.

So could Ronnie. Only he'd have to do it

now, before it got any darker, and someone came up to check he'd done the black-out properly.

He opened the window.

8 ✢ Second Strike

Now that he was sitting astride the window-sill, it seemed a very long way down. There was a drainpipe, a foot to the left of the window; he could slither down that to the lavatory roof, and from there he could jump to the top of the Anderson shelter. As long as no one was looking out of the kitchen window...

This was the hardest bit. He swung his other leg over, so that he was sitting on the window-sill facing out. He'd already turned off the lamp and closed the door to the upstairs landing, so that no one would see a light showing and come to report it.

Now, if he was going to do it, he had to make a decisive move - there would be no going back once he did. He would have to turn himself backwards and then drop down below the window-sill, hanging by his hands, and at the same time reach across for the pipe. He contemplated the gap. If he missed... well, there would be a painful slither down to the tiled roof and, if he couldn't get his balance in time, from there to the ground. He might hurt himself but it wasn't a big enough drop to give him a serious injury.

He was still sitting on the window-sill, clinging on hard with both hands. The bottom edge of the frame pressed painfully into his legs. If he was going to do it, it must be now, before it got any darker...

He took a deep breath. Now...

And he was hanging in space, fingernails clawing the wooden frame, legs flailing. He forced himself to let go with one hand, grabbing wildly at the downpipe. One foot struck it with such a clang that if anyone had been in the kitchen they'd have been sure to hear. Swinging like a monkey from a branch, he lurched across and clamped himself against the pipe. He'd imagined himself climbing down gradually as you might scale down a rope, but the pipe wasn't flexible like rope and he was unable to grip it. He slithered much faster than he intended, hit the roof and struggled for balance on its down-slope.

Half-way. He'd grazed his knees against the wall, but he'd made it. The next bit was easier. He let go of the pipe, judged the distance - flung himself forward, arms stretched out, and landed sprawling with a faceful of earth on top of the Anderson.

He was winded, but free. He jumped off the shelter roof, the side farthest from the house, and let himself out of the back garden gate to the alleyway beyond.

He brushed soil from his clothes and tried to look nonchalant as he strolled into the street, hoping he wouldn't meet anyone he knew. It was strange, being out at this time of evening in the black-out. The streets were darkening fast, with no lighted windows. The unlit street-lamps were like barren trees, black stalks. The searchlights came on as he walked – cones of light, criss-crossing the sky.

Damn! He should have brought something for Dusty to eat – if only he could have got downstairs to the larder. There had been some of Mum's squashed-fly biscuits, and perhaps a spare Eccles cake. Tomorrow, perhaps... That's if Dusty was where Ronnie thought he was. But now he felt sure enough to bet money on it, if he'd had any money.

He broke into a jog as he reached Gordon Street, his eyes scanning the gloom for anything that might trip him up. Two people passed him, walking the other way, shining a feeble torch-beam down at the pavement. Ronnie wished he had a torch – it would be hard to find his way to the stables. Hurry up, while there was still a glimmer of daylight left...

It was the smell that alerted him. A country smell of straw and dung, and a gap to his left. He turned into Red Lion Yard, walking carefully over the uneven flagstones towards the stable at the back corner.

"Dusty? Are you there?"

He heard a breathy whickering, and the white blaze of the horse's face lifted like a tattered flag against the window.

"Good boy, Lucky!" Ronnie went to him, and slid back the bolt of the door. He heard a scuffling in the straw, too loud for rats or mice.

"Who's that?" wavered a voice.

"Dusty? It's only me, Ronnie." He could make out Dusty's pale face as he scrambled to his feet.

"Is this where you sleep? In the stable, with him?" Ronnie said, with a hand against the horse's warm neck.

"Yes! I like it. I slept here last night. It's nice and warm, better than that old ruin."

"What, all through the raid? Didn't you go to the street shelter?"

"No, I stayed with Lucky."

"Does Alf know?"

"No! You won't tell him? He came round about five o'clock, then he went to the pub. But he comes really early in the morning, to do his rounds. Lucky's as good as an alarm-clock – he neighs as soon as he sees Alf at the street corner. Then I nip round behind the straw-stack." Dusty's feet moved in the horse's bedding. "Look – I'm sorry about yesterday. Running off like that."

"Never mind that." Was it only yesterday? It seemed like a week ago. Ronnie remembered Miss Flitwick-Price. "Did you know there's this woman looking for you? Evacuation Officer? She came round our house."

"You didn't tell her?"

"Well, what *could* I tell her, even if I wanted to? I had to tell her I'd seen you, 'cos someone had seen us at the market. But I didn't know you were here, did I?"

"She won't find me." Dusty sounded doubtful. "Not if I stay hidden, if I don't go to the market any more, or the canteens, where someone might see me – "

"You can live on horse food, I suppose!"

Ronnie was sarcastic, but Dusty answered

quite seriously, "I've tried it. It's not that bad, oats and stuff – if you split the grains, 'cos otherwise it's a bit husky. Alf keeps it in a bin, through there." He pointed at the adjoining stable. "And there's a water-pump out in the yard. I haven't tried eating hay."

Ronnie burst out laughing. "You're crackers!"

"No, I'm not! I like horses so I don't mind sharing their food. I want to be a jockey," Dusty said.

Ronnie almost said, "I'm going to be a Spitfire pilot," but he remembered Dusty's father and swallowed the words before they got out. Instead he said, "Who needs jockeys in wartime?"

"I meant after the war," Dusty said, but his voice was doubtful as he added, "That is, if we win. What if we don't?"

"'Course we'll win." Ronnie said it automatically, but then he thought: who's winning at the moment? *We're* not, with houses and factories smashed to bits every night. "Look," he said, "I'll try and bring you some food in the morning, all right? Bread and dripping or something. I'll have to get back. I'm in trouble already, and that's before they know I sneaked out."

"See you tomorrow, then, Ronnie." Dusty sounded wistful.

"Go to the shelter, if there's a raid!" Ronnie told him sternly. "You know where the street shelter is, don't you? Out there, turn left. See you."

Ronnie hadn't made it past the heap of rubble that was the Red Lion when the siren started, with its sickening rise and fall. Damn! An early raid, tonight of all nights! Now what should he do? Belt it for home, or go in the street shelter with Dusty? He expected to hear Dusty's feet running towards him, but there was no sound from the direction of the stable. He turned and ran back.

"Come on! The street shelter, I told you! You only get about two minutes!"

"I'm not going." Dusty's voice came from floor level. "I can't leave Lucky."

"Don't be stupid!"

"I won't," Dusty repeated obstinately. "You heard what Alf said, didn't you? About lightning never striking the same place twice? And besides, his name's Lucky?"

Ronnie hauled the door open, went inside and groped for Dusty's arm in the darkness.

"Get up! You're wasting time!"

"You go." The boy's voice was muffled against the horse's legs. "I'm not leaving him."

Ronnie straightened. He could hear the stuttering of ack-ack guns, and the drone of aircraft. And beside him, quite incongruous, the comforting sound of Lucky chomping hay, contented as a cow chewing the cud.

"We can't take him with us. Can you imagine?" His voice wavered.

"What's *funny*?"

"I was just thinking of taking him to the Underground, down the escalator – " It had come into his mind like a cartoon picture, Lucky riding down, sitting back on his haunches, everyone staring... But here they were, he and Dusty, laughing like a pair of drunks, with the sirens wailing and Jerry aircraft overhead...

It's not my fault, Ronnie thought. I tried! He knew it wasn't really safer here, with the warm smells of horse and hay, but it was easy to think so. "If you're not going, then neither am I," he said firmly, and leaned against Lucky's warm flank.

It had been dark ten minutes ago, but it wasn't dark now. Looking out, Ronnie saw the white lights of parachute flares, like fireworks. He heard the dull boom of an explosion, and slowly the sky turned pink, flushing the underneaths of the clouds, like a late, glorious sunset.

"I'm going out to look," he told Dusty. "It wasn't very close, that one – "

But the next one was. He didn't even hear the aircraft overhead or the whine of the bomb, but as he turned to bolt the door behind him a blast wave almost knocked him off his feet. His mouth must have opened of its own accord; although his ears were numb, he slowly registered sounds – the frightened scraping of Lucky's hooves on the stable floor, Dusty's voice soothing him. And now he could not only hear but see – golden light reflected in the horse's bulging eyes, Dusty's face lit up like an angel's in a painting. Ronnie pulled himself to his feet.

The entrance to the yard was a wall of smoke. He heard the *crack, crack* of anti-aircraft guns; heard the whistle of shrapnel as it rained down like hail. He smelled burning, heard the horse's churning hooves.

"Get him out!" he yelled. "Incendiaries! This whole place'll go up – all that hay and straw and wood!"

He flung the door open wide. Lucky was cowering against the back wall, feet braced, eyes goggling. Ronnie's eyes stung; he heard

Dusty coughing.

"Get him out!" he yelled again. He ran to the adjoining stable, where Alf kept Lucky's harness. No time for a bridle – he grabbed the rope halter. And then he saw a burning fragment drop through from the hay-loft above to land on the straw-stack. At once the greedy flame snatched at the dry straw, licking, spreading. Ronnie yanked off his jacket and flung it over the flames, but the fire was too quick, devouring new straw faster than he could suffocate it. It was no good. He coughed and spluttered, his eyes streaming. He ran back, snatched Lucky's water-bucket and hurled its contents over the flames. And that was it. All the water gone. The fire faltered for just a second, then leaped on across the stack. One patch of damp wasn't going to halt its progress. The wooden spars between the two stables were glowing, smouldering, ready to leap into fire.

"He won't come! He's too frightened!" Dusty gasped.

The flames were already lapping at the straw at the front of the stable. A second more and there'd be a wall of fire, barricading the horse inside. Ronnie kicked the straw away in a shower of sparks, ran to Lucky and thrust the rope halter on to his head.

"Come on, boy! Move! You've got to – "
He pulled as hard as he could. The horse only tugged back, leaning all his weight against the wall behind. He saw everything as an enemy now – the fire, the two boys, the smoke outside – it was reflected in his huge, staring eyes. He snorted, his nostrils wide and flared.

"Make him! Make him move!" Dusty screamed, in an agony of frustration.

Sweat ran into Ronnie's eyes. Heat fanned his face. Any second now, and they'd have to leave him or be burned alive, all three of them... Ronnie caught Dusty's hysteria, and tried to whack the horse with the end of the halter rope. Dusty, seeing, grabbed one of the wooden spars and snapped it off, then ran round behind Lucky and gave him a resounding thwack on the rump. "Move, you stupid horse! Get out!" He whacked again, and again, with surprising force. Lucky quivered, then leaped forward and surged out of the open door, dragging Ronnie with him. Ronnie turned round to make sure Dusty was following, and they all three plunged on into the wall of smoke.

9 ✣ Evacuee

Ronnie tottered forward, choking. Lucky, having burst out with such determination, now dragged at his rope; he snorted at every step, smelling the smoke and explosive, placing his feet like a horse trying to skate on ice. But they were out. Behind them, the fire finally took hold; the straw-stack went up like Bonfire Night, with a fierce crackle. The blaze threw long shadows across the yard.

"Dusty! You all right?" Ronnie yelled.

"I'm here!" Dusty was stumbling behind.

The street, almost deserted half an hour ago, was now alive with frantic activity. Through the smoke pall, Ronnie made out a fire tender and a Heavy Rescue lorry, and figures dashing about, and firemen aiming hoses at the houses opposite the pub. Fire leaped from the windows of the upper storeys. As far as Ronnie could see, one section of the terrace had simply gone.

"Blimey!"

He'd seen bomb damage enough times, but not this – complete obliteration. No one was even bothering with the fires in Red Lion Yard. There was more urgent business to attend to. Lucky's nerve, which had got him this far, failed him now – he threw up his head with a snort of disbelief, yanking the halter rope and Ronnie's arm at the end of it.

"Where shall we take him? The milk depot?" Dusty asked. But the road was completely blocked, everywhere a swirl of smoke and dust and noise – nowhere was safe for a horse tonight. If the ack-ack guns started up again, there'd be steel shrapnel rain... Without Lucky, Ronnie would have aimed for the nearest Underground station.

A figure loomed up. "Christ Almighty – a horse, and a couple of kids! What the hell do you think you're doing, out in this lot?"

And then another voice shouted out, "Oi, mate! Is this your'n?" and a stumpy figure broke away from the policeman who'd been restraining him, and hobbled up as fast as he could.

Alf.

He flung his arms round the horse's neck.

"Lucky, Lucky, me old mate! You're here, God alone knows how!" Then his shoulders heaved, and he wiped his eyes with the horse's mane. Ronnie's eyes blurred too as he realised that Alf must have seen the stable ablaze and thought Lucky was still inside.

"Get that horse out of here!" yelled a fireman. "There's another tender coming – "

"Where? Where's there another stable?" Ronnie shouted to Alf.

"Round by the depot. I'll take him there." Alf took hold of Lucky's halter rope, then looked closely at the boys. "You're heroes, the three of you – "

"Get out of the road! You boys, into the shelter. Now!" The policeman shoved them along the street.

Dusty looked anxiously at the shambling figure of Alf, taking a detour down an alleyway to find a way back to the depot. "Will he be all right?"

"I hope so," Ronnie said. But who could guarantee anyone's safety, in this?

* * * * *

"You could have been killed," Mum said again and again. She kept looking at Ronnie as if to convince herself that he hadn't been.

He and Dusty sat side by side at the table, with bowls of porridge and mugs of tea. Dusty was eating very awkwardly, with both hands bandaged. He hadn't noticed the burns on his hands until he was inside the shelter.

It was Dad who had found them there – desperate with worry when he heard that Ronnie had disappeared, he'd had to help with a rescue in his own area before going to look for him. They arrived home, the three of them, in the early dawn – all of them filthy, caked with dust and ash. "These lads smell like a pair of smoked kippers!" Dad said, and Mum had fetched the tin bath. Now they were both clean and washed, and Dusty wore spare clothes of Ronnie's. Patsy, from Nan's armchair, eyed them with surprise, as if Ronnie had turned into twins.

"Ronnie," Dusty whispered, when Mum went into the kitchen to refill the teapot. "You know I told you about my dad? Being a Spitfire pilot?" He gazed at Ronnie, pleading. "It's not true. I made it up."

"I know," Ronnie said. "Miss Flitty-Whatsit told us." And that was the end of the conversation. Patsy's mouth opened in a long, determined wail and Mum came back in to hush her, as Nan was still asleep upstairs.

"Now, bed," Mum said firmly, as soon as they'd finished eating. Dusty protested that he wasn't tired, but Ronnie was yawning. Mum wasn't taking no for an answer, and soon Dusty was installed in Ronnie's camp-bed downstairs while Ronnie went up to his parents' room. Much later, in the middle of the morning, there was a second breakfast downstairs. Ronnie looked suspiciously at Mum, who should have been at the rest centre hours ago.

"I'm not letting you out of my sight," she said, reading his glance. "Nor your friend here."

Miss Flitwick-Price would be told, Ronnie knew. There was no chance of Dusty walking out of here, back to his life on the streets.

"I want a word with you, young man," Nan said sharply to Dusty, when the plates were cleared. "In the garden. Now."

Dusty looked startled, but followed her. Washing up at the kitchen sink, Ronnie could see them talking, on and on – at least Nan talked, while Dusty looked more and more shame-faced and upset. When at last they came back inside, Ronnie could see that Dusty had been crying.

* * * * *

Ronnie sat alone in the train compartment. He wasn't used to feeling so smart: he was dressed in clean school clothes, and Mum had trimmed his hair and slicked it down with water and even put some of Dad's Brylcreem on it. His cardboard suitcase was on the rack overhead, with his label on it (he refused to actually wear the label, as if he were five years old), and his gas-mask in its case was slung over his shoulder. Otherwise, it wasn't really much like last time – then, he'd been in a carriage full of excited or nervous children, and he hadn't known where he was going.

This time, he did know. He was going to Newton Abbot, back to join his class-mates and teachers. Miss Flitwick-Price had found him a billet with one of the other boys from his class – not Chalky, to his disappointment. "Just as well," Mum said drily. "I'm sending you down there so's you stay out of mischief, not to find more." And Dusty was going back to Somerset, too, so they wouldn't be all that far apart and might even be able to meet each other. He had Dusty's evacuation address, and Mum had given him a book of stamps and some notepaper.

He wished they could have travelled down together; Dusty's stop was on the same line. First, though, Dusty was going home to Leytonstone. He was going to see his father. That was all Nan's doing. In the garden, Dusty had been given the full treatment – the story of Grandad, and the nightmares, and the terrible stretch of no-man's-land, and the terror that could last a man's whole life. Nan had left Dusty in no doubt that his father deserved understanding and admiration, not contempt.

She was a good'un, Nan was. In Ronnie's pocket was the stick of humbug she'd given him at Paddington. When would he see her again? And Mum, and Dad, and Patsy? "Can't we all go down to Devon?" he'd asked.

"Of course not. Dad's got his work here – important work!" Mum said.

Dad was a hero. No one had called him that, but Ronnie knew he was. Last night, he'd torn his hands burrowing under smashed wood and masonry to pull out a woman trapped next to her kitchen stove. She'd have burned by the time the rescue services arrived. As it was, she was at the rest centre with her little girl.

It was an odd thing, this hero business. Alf had told Ronnie he was a hero, but he hadn't felt like one. And it wasn't really him who'd saved Lucky. If it had been up to him, Dusty would have come to the street shelter and Lucky would have died. And without Dusty's inspiration – grabbing the spar, even though it burned his hands – they'd never have got Lucky out. Dusty would never have left the horse; he'd have died with him rather than leave. So who was the hero?

Ronnie gazed out of the train window at green rolling fields, and at trees decked in rich autumn colours, gold and bronze. Far above he saw a vapour trail of smoke, high in the blue. He thought enviously of the pilot. If the war was still on when he was eighteen, that's what he was going to be. It wasn't all shooting down Jerries and collecting medals and being photographed grinning for the newspapers, he knew that. But to be up there, at the controls of a plane... instead of down in the London streets, wondering what was going to land on you... it must be amazing! Even for Dusty's dad, it must have been amazing for some of the time.

The train was running alongside a river estuary – a shining expanse of mud, all dotted with gulls and wading birds. Newton Abbot was a little way inland, but when he got out of the train he might still be able to smell the sea. And he'd be able to sleep in bed all night long, and not have to squat in a smelly shelter, wondering if the next bomb had Ronald Cooper inscribed on it.

The train slowed, and pulled into a station. All the name-boards had been taken down, but he knew it was the right one because Miss Flitwick-

Price had told him how many stops to count.

As he got down, lugging his case, he saw that everyone from school had come on to the platform to meet him. Mr Fordson, their teacher; and Chalky White, freckled and grinning with his tie all lopsided; and Meg Coombes who said she was going to marry Ronnie when she was grown-up; and Frankie Phillips, with his mouth hanging open as usual; and Jonno and Ken, and lots of others who were more interested in the chocolate machine.

"About time," said Chalky, giving him a friendly punch. "What kept you?"

Further Reading

Bernard Ashley, *Johnnie's Blitz*; (Viking, 1995) Puffin

Nina Bawden, *Carrie's War*; (Gollancz, 1973) Puffin

David Rees, *The Exeter Blitz*; Hamish Hamilton, 1978

Adèle Geras, *Candle in the Dark*; A & C Black, 1995

Dennis Hamley, *The War and Freddy*; Scholastic, 1994

Dennis Hamley, *Flying Bombs*; Watts, 1998

Judith Kerr, *When Hitler Stole Pink Rabbit*; Collins, 1971

Michelle Magorian, *Goodnight Mister Tom*; (Viking, 1981) Puffin

Terrance Dicks, *Spitfire Summer*; Piccadilly, 1991

Jean Ure, *Big Tom*; Collins, 2000

Robert Westall, *Blitzcat*; Macmillan, 1989

Robert Westall, *The Kingdom by the Sea*; (Methuen, 1990) Mammoth

Robert Westall, *The Machine-Gunners*; Macmillan, 1975

For older readers

Michelle Magorian, *A Little Love Song* (Methuen, 1991) Mammoth

Linda Newbery, *The Shouting Wind*; Collins, 1995

Jill Paton Walsh, *Fireweed*; (Macmillan, 1978) Puffin